THE HOLIDAY ARRANGEMENT

DINEEN MILLER

CHAPTER 1

Despite the pleasant drop in temperature and humidity, the late November air held the familiar scent of Siesta Key Beach, just a few miles away from downtown Sarasota. Jeremy Payne made a mental note to walk the shore Saturday morning.

Noticing his friend cleaning up the remnants of his lunch, he finished the last bite of his burger. "Time to walk."

They gathered sacks and drink cups from the bench at the far side of a courtyard between several shops and a couple of small restaurants.

"Hey, we're throwing a Christmas party, so put it on your calendar." Stephen waited for him to reply with his goofball expression that always reminded him of the actor Kevin James.

Jeremy tossed the remnants of his lunch into the receptacle. A quick burger and fries with his best friend defined his social life these days. His friend knew it. So did his wife.

"Who's asking? You or Allison?"

Stephen took a sip from his soda before tossing it into the garbage as well. "Me, of course." He shrugged. "And Allison."

"I knew it. Thanks, but no thanks. Not interested in another setup."

Stephen held his hands up in mock innocence. "I swear that's not what this is. Allison has always dreamed of hosting a big Christmas party and now that we're settled in our new house, she's swung into full gear."

"But Thanksgiving is next week." They stopped in front of a shop whose front window display boasted Christmas ornaments, miniature trees, and gift boxes with bright red and green bows.

"Christmas has already arrived, in case you didn't notice." Stephen tapped on the window to make his point, then waved apologetically to the clerk whose attention he'd caught. "She's planning it for early December so that more people will be free to come. Before all the office and family parties hit."

"That's a couple of weeks away." Jeremy pushed the crosswalk button.

"That's why I'm asking you now. Allison wants a bunch of people there. And as her husband, I'm obliged to help make her dream come true."

Jeremy laughed. "So that's what I am now? Just a warm body to help fulfill your wife's dream?" The crossing light turned green.

"Come on. Please? I was serious when I said this wasn't a setup. Just a bunch of friends getting together to celebrate Christmas. Besides, Allison learned her lesson after the last debacle that resulted from her attempts at playing matchmaker."

He dearly hoped so. Probably the most awkward moment of his life to date. He'd never forget the smell of burning polyester for as long as he lived. "About time."

"And she's truly sorry. She had no idea the woman was on the nutty side."

Jeremy stopped and gave Stephen his 'you've-got-to-be-kidding-me' stare. "Did she even know the woman?"

Stephen hunched his shoulders as he lifted his hands. "Kind of."

Jeremy waved him off. "No dice. Count me out."

They'd walked the full length of Main Street in downtown Sarasota and turned around. Their normal routine to justify eating a greasy burger and fries.

"Tell Allison I appreciate the invite. Tell her I have plans or something."

"Do you?"

He hesitated, searching his mental calendar for any commitments. Since his breakup with Sheridan, his social calendar had tanked big time. Guess their years together didn't garner him much loyalty in their social circle. Didn't help much that she'd controlled that aspect of their image in an attempt to become a power couple in the local society. Another reason why they were better off going their separate ways.

"Just come and hang out with your best friend then." Stephen rested his hands on his chest, brows raised and a goofy grin on his face.

He quickened his speed at the next crosswalk to beat the flashing hand, warning him the light was about to change. Maybe that's what he needed, a *life* change. "Who's going to be there?"

"Just friends. I swear. A few neighbors. Allison's best friend, Corinne—"

Jeremy shot him a suspicious look. It was bad enough that his mother kept trying to set him up with the recently divorced women in her church. He didn't need any more surprise setups or one of those just-happened-to-stop-by sideswipes.

Stephen held his hand out. "Trust me. Allison would never set you up with her best friend."

Jeremy stopped in front of his building and turned to his friend. "So I'm good enough for psycho woman but not her best friend?" Why did he even care?

Stephen frowned at him. "No, that's not it at all. It crosses some agreement they made a few years ago." He paused. "What, are you secretly wanting to be set up?"

"No." Jeremy shook his head and headed to the entrance of his building. Stephen's building was another twenty feet down the walk. He was better off alone, at least for a while. He needed time to figure out what he really wanted out of life. Sheridan had called the shots for so long that he didn't realize how far off course his ship had sailed until too late.

Stephen's voice followed him inside. "Just think about it. You can stop in, have a couple hors d'oeuvre, and leave."

❄

CORINNE CARTER WAITED for her mother to sit down at the table before taking the seat opposite her. The restaurant buzzed with the noon crowd. "What did you think I meant?"

Her mother scooted closer to the table. "I don't know. I thought maybe you had a date."

Corinne laughed. "Mom, don't start. I just got settled into my condo and have yet to even meet my neighbors. Let your daughter breathe a little first, okay? Dating is the last thing on my mind right now."

She shook out the cloth napkin and draped it over her lap as the server filled their glasses with ice water. A long drink pushed away the heat of the day. She'd forgotten how warm Florida could still be in late November. Another thing she'd have to readjust to.

"All right. Fine. I'm just trying to help. You've been alone for a while now—"

"Like I said before, being alone doesn't—"

"Doesn't mean you're lonely. Yes, yes, I remember. I just want to see you happy."

She reached out and took her mother's hand, waiting for her to look up from her study of the menu and meet Corinne's gaze. "Mom, I am happy. I'm back in Sarasota, near the best beaches in the world. And my mother."

Her mother gave her a sly grin. "And in that order, I presume."

Corinne dropped her chin in mock despair. "Oy vey."

Her mother covered her mouth as she giggled before turning serious. "I'm so sorry things didn't work out with you and Peter."

Corinne studied her menu as an excuse to keep her eyes diverted. The last thing she wanted her mother to see were the tears she'd yet to shed over her divorce. Their marriage had ended long before the papers had been signed—and they were separated for a good year before that— but the sting of failure still lingered. "It's for the best, Mom. Peter and I both agreed we did our best. Now we both get a fresh start. I even took back my maiden name."

"Good." Her mother smiled and diverted her attention to her own menu.

She still hadn't told her mother about Peter's alcoholism. The years of living in denial. The repetitive roller coaster of rehab and relapse had left her with enough shame to choke a herd of horses. Plus, she'd grown tired of the pity-filled looks from friends and conversations that inevitably circled the circumstantial drain of their failed marriage.

She gulped down half of her water. Moving back to Sarasota really was her chance to start over. Alone. For the first time in her life, she could give her full attention to her marketing career. And in no way did she miss California traffic.

The server returned to their table and took their orders, leaving them to munch on the bread and butter. Corinne tore off one small piece, allowing herself to have a small dose of carbs.

"Have you made plans for Christmas?" Her mother dipped her knife into the butter pat on the table and spread a generous portion on the chunk of bread in her hand. Somehow her mother managed to eat large amounts of bread yet remain thin as a rail. A trait she didn't inherit.

"Just to be with you."

"No company parties?"

"Not that I know of yet. I'll know more once I start on Monday."

"That could be a great way to meet someone."

"Mom, please."

Her mother shrugged. "I'm just saying…"

"I'm not interested in meeting anyone right now."

The server set plates of food in front of them. Corinne dipped a spoon into the bowl of lobster bisque nestled against a salad.

"Are you sure, sweetie?"

"About what?" Creamy goodness exploded over her tongue.

"Meeting someone." Her mother's expression turned evasive, which usually happened when she'd done something without permission. Margaret Carter had a notorious reputation for trying to fix things, especially other people's lives. Corinne had learned to circumvent her mother's tampering as a teenager, so when she and Peter moved to California, she'd breathed a guilty sigh of relief for many years.

Corinne put down her spoon. "Mom, what did you do? Did you set me up?"

"No, of course not." Her mother studied her food. "That's up to the matchmaker."

"The what?!" Her shout brought the full attention of the table of four to their right. She gave them an apologetic smile. "Sorry." Corinne leaned forward, careful to keep her voice to a rough whisper. "Did you say *matchmaker*?"

Her mother gave her a demure nod.

"Mother, why would you do that?! We're not technically Jewish."

Her mother held her hands out. "She's not Jewish. She's Indian, but she said she can work with us."

CHAPTER 2

The splashes of red that Corinne had noticed when she drove up to Allison's place turned out to be small poinsettias in green pots lining the walkway. Twinkle lights, pine cones, and sparkling red ribbon embellished a garland trimming the double doors, which boasted two oversized Christmas wreaths adorned in a similar fashion.

She had to hand it to Allison. The woman knew how to decorate for the holidays. She pushed the bell, which played a short snippet of Jingle Bells. Corinne resisted rolling her eyes as Allison opened the door.

Allison squealed as she wrapped Corinne in a hug. "You're here! My best friend is back."

Corinne laughed. "I've been back for over a month."

"I know, but it's still sinking in." Allison tugged her into the house.

She gasped at her first glimpse of Allison's home. Christmas baubles and snow globes covered every surface. A nine-foot tree filled one corner of the living area, decorated with a chartreuse green ribbon boasting bright red polka dots. Matching green and red glitter balls dotted the tree along with a plethora of glass icicles. White twinkle lights strobed softly to complete the effect. Just add a soft lens and voilà!

"Wow… Allison, this is amazing." She felt like a kid who stepped into a real-life North Pole setting in a snow globe. "How long have you been working on this?"

"Days. And some nights. But it'll be worth it. Everyone is going to have a fabulous time. I even hired performers."

"You what?" She followed Allison to the formal dining room table. Cakes, cookies, and Christmas candies covered the table in a cluttered mass of sweet delights. She grabbed a red foil-wrapped chocolate kiss and popped it into her mouth.

Allison swatted her hand with a light tap. "Hey now! The party hasn't started yet."

Corinne pointed to her mouth and mumbled over the chocolaty goodness covering her tongue. "It has in here." She swallowed and laughed with her friend. "So why did you want me to come so early, anyway?"

"Because we need to get dressed." Allison grabbed her wrist and started dragging her toward the master suite.

"Wait. What? I am dressed." She glanced down at her red paisley tie-at-the-waist shirt, black capris, and cork wedge heels with black straps. "I already look Christmasy, Allison."

Her friend stopped and batted mock innocent eyes at her. "Didn't I tell you? It's a Christmas costume party."

AFTER TWEAKING HIS SANTA HAT, Jeremy rang the doorbell. He groaned inwardly as Jingle Bells played, announcing his presence. When Stephen had told him to wear a costume, Jeremy had just laughed at him. Another good reason not to go, but then Stephen played the best friend card again after calling him a scrooge. That just pushed Jeremy to prove him wrong.

He glanced down at his jeans and green Hawaiian shirt with the words "Mele Kalikimaka" intermingled with white Christmas trees, palm trees, and hula girls. That's as much costume as he could muster.

And red socks.

Besides, Jeremy never could turn down a friend in need, and Stephen seemed to really want him present, although he wouldn't say why. He'd never seen Stephen act so "needy," come to think of it. Maybe the party would loosen his friend's tongue.

A cute elf with curled shoes that sprouted bells at the end swung open the door. "Welcome to the party!" She bobbed her head, which made the bell on the end of her stiff pointy hat jingle as well. Her costume reminded him of the grumpy girl elf in the movie *A Christmas Story*. "You're just in time…" she eyed his shirt, "Hawaiian Santa?"

Jeremy gave her a slow grin. "Very good." He tilted his head and pointed at her. "A Christmas Story?"

She giggled. "You're the first one to get it. My dad loves that movie so I thought, why not?"

That movie defined his childhood. Now he felt old. Wait… her father? He felt his grin slip a bit. When did Stephen's oldest daughter grow up? "Katie?"

She giggled again. "Yeah, I didn't think you recognized me."

"I didn't. Now I do. Last time I saw you, you had—"

"Braces and pigtails. I start college in the fall."

"Wow, that happened fast."

"Dad's in the backyard by the grill." She stepped back and swung her hand to invite him in.

"Thanks." He smiled and slipped by her, relieved he'd recognized Katie and avoided a very embarrassing scenario. Not that he had any interest and dating someone younger than him—Sheridan's ten-year difference had felt more like twenty sometimes. And these days, he had a hard time judging women's ages.

He headed to the lanai area. The sooner he got his friend talking and had an hors d'oeuvre, the sooner he could leave.

As he stepped into the house, two costumed guests came rushing down the hall right in his direction. He recognized Allison right away. Then took note of the woman she dragged behind her, dressed as Mrs. Claus.

He'd ream Stephen good when he had a chance for the set-up his wife was about to push on him.

✳

ALLISON FLUFFED the white fur trim of Corinne's costume. "I knew you'd look good in this."

Corinne frowned at her reflection. "I look like an overstuffed strawberry Pop-Tart with icing. Seriously, Allison, Mrs. Claus? Way to make a girl feel old."

"Old?" Allison actually looked offended. "I think you look sexy."

She rolled her eyes. "That's just gross. You know that, right?" She started to undo the belt.

Allison stopped her. "No, no, no, please wear it?"

"Why? What I had on was festive enough."

"For me?" Allison sported her famous pouty face, which always succeeded in getting what she wanted—in high school and college. They hadn't called her the blonde bombshell for nothing.

But something seemed off with her best friend. "Allie, what's going on?" She tugged her to the bench in front of the massive king-sized platform bed.

Allison wiggled around in the pink tight dress of her Cindy Lou Who costume. Corinne couldn't wait to see Stephen dressed as her counterpart, the Grinch.

"Is something going on between you and Stephen?"

One of Allison's red pigtail bows fell out. Tears filled her eyes. "Since we moved into the house, Stephen works all the time. He's hardly home for dinner either." Her face bunched into a tortured mass of tears and sobs. "And he just hired a new secretary who's like right out of college. And blonde!"

Corinne hugged her. "I'm sure Stephen's just busy at work right now."

Allie popped off the bench to grab tissues, which she promptly filled with more tears and blubbering. "I don't know… you think so?"

She stood and turned Allie around to face the full-length mirror. Her costume highlighted her curves to perfection. "Hey, have you looked at you? Allie, you're amazing."

Allison shot her a sarcastic expression and pointed to her raccoon eyes.

The doorbell rang as she grabbed a makeup cloth. "Your guests are arriving so let's get you cleaned up and get this party started."

By the time she got Allie cleaned up, there was no time to change back into her own clothes. She'd have to just suck it up and be the Claus. Missus, that is. She buckled the black belt as Allie tugged on her matching slippers and stood.

"Do I look okay?"

The woman could wear potato sacks and look like Coco Chanel. "Stunning. Ready?"

"Oh, wait." Allie grabbed a lipstick from her vanity and grabbed Corinne's chin.

Before Corinne could push her away, Allie had coated her lips with candy apple red lipstick. She frowned at her reflection. Applied to perfection—how did the woman do that?—and as red as her costume.

"There. That's perfect." Allie grinned from ear to ear and batted her inch-long fake lashes. "You look amazing."

"But it's so… red."

"I know. Matches your costume." She grabbed Corinne's hand and tugged her out of the bedroom into the main part of the house. People had started to arrive and mingle around the food table and outside on the lanai.

"Hurry." Allison did as much of a dash as she could in her tight dress.

Corrine's black boots tapped on the tile. As they hit the foyer and living room, a guy in a Hawaiian shirt and a Santa hat walked in. Another quick study and she recognized the pattern—hula girls and palm trees. Typical Florida costume. She tried not to roll her eyes.

Allison stopped in front of him. "Hey, Jeremy! You made it. Have you seen Stephen?"

"No, but Katie said he's by the grill."

"Great." She glanced at Corinne. "I don't think you've met my best friend, Corinne. She just moved back to Sarasota a month ago."

Something about him looked super familiar. He had just a light dusting of gray at his temples and looked like he exercised regularly. And then her mind unlocked a memory all the way back to high school.

Long hair, T-shirts… "Jeremy Payne?"

He did a double-take. "Cori?"

CHAPTER 3

A flood of memories rushed in all at once. Waiting by the lockers for Cori to put her books away so they could walk together to the cafeteria. Hanging out at Friday night games. Going to the movies with friends. And then the graduation party they ditched to walk the beach.

He shook himself back to reality. "I didn't know you moved back?"

She smiled as she nodded. "Yeah, just a month ago."

Allison glanced between them. "You guys know each other?"

Cori cleared her throat. "Yeah, we were best friends in high school."

"Him?" Allison pointed her thumb at him with an expression of disbelief.

"Hey now." Jeremy frowned at her.

Allison giggled behind her hand. Just like he'd seen Katie do. "I'm just kidding." She bounced her gaze between them. "I need to find Stephen, so I'm enlisting you two as the welcoming committee."

Jeremy started to protest, but Cori smiled and said sure.

An awkward silence hovered between them as Allison dashed off.

Cori busied herself adjusting the buckle of her costume.

Jeremy tucked his hands into his jeans pockets. "So Cori, did I hear you moved to California—with your husband, right?" Could he sound more obvious?

Her head shot up. "Yes, Peter. But we're not together anymore."

"Oh, I'm sorry."

"Don't be. We agreed we did our best, but it just wasn't working. Hadn't for a long time."

She stood there, staring at him as if she expected him to say something.

Why did he feel so awkward around her, like he was back in high school again. He'd grown comfortable with himself and didn't have to work hard to find a date, if he even wanted one. Though after Sheridan, he was in no hurry to jump back into anything. Maybe he just needed a friend more than anything.

"That's good, right? Sometimes it's best to go separate ways."

She tilted her head. "Sounds like you're speaking from experience."

"Yes, last year. It was either get engaged or get a new life. We just wanted different things."

"Together long?"

"Kind of."

"You may as well have been married then." She laughed and then covered her mouth. "I'm sorry. That wasn't very thoughtful."

Jeremy laughed. Some things didn't change. Cori always did speak her mind and then consider her words later. "It's okay. Long story."

She gave him a smile filled with the warmth and compassion he remembered the first time he asked her out. "It's really great to see you again, Jeremy."

Before he could respond, the doorbell rang. Cori jumped to answer, becoming a cordial Christmas hostess.

And he couldn't tear his gaze away to even see who was at the door. His words 'great to see you too' fell into the abyss of the past. And probably for the best, because he enjoyed seeing her just a little more than he should.

❄

CORINNE FOUND Allison sitting at one of the decorated tables out on the lanai. A cold front had moved through during the previous night, so the temperature had dropped into the upper sixties halfway through the evening, which made the party seem more festive and relieved the heat generated by her faux fur collar. She had to keep blowing the fuzz away from her mouth.

She plopped down on the chair. "I think I've officially greeted every guest for you."

"Thanks."

She did a sweep of the guests and the grill area, but no sign of Allie's husband. "Where's Stephen?"

"He had to go to work."

"What? I thought he was manning the grill."

"He handed it off to Jeremy." Allison's chin quivered. She took a drink from a plastic cup with Christmas wreaths printed on the sides. Judging by the milky substance it contained, Corinne guessed it to be egg nog. She took the cup and smelled it.

"You spiked it, didn't you?"

Allie took a sip and nodded. "Yep, and I'm not sorry for it either, because you know what? My husband's having an affair."

Corinne could tell Allie was feeling the drink. She took the cup and tossed the rest into the grass.

"Hey, I wasn't finished with that." Allie's last word slurred a bit.

How much had she drunk? She stood and tugged Allie to her feet. "Okay, let's get you inside and get some coffee in you."

As they passed the sweets table, Allie put her hand to mouth. "I think I'm going to be sick."

Allie would be mortified if she puked in front of all her guests. Corinne put her arm around Allison's waist and led her down the hall as fast as she could keep the woman moving. She thought they'd made it, but as soon as they stepped into the bedroom, Allie puked everything she drank.

All over Corinne's costume.

CHAPTER 4

The party had dwindled so Jeremy turned off the grill and headed back into the house. He placed the platter of burgers and hotdogs on the counter with the rest of the fixings.

Stephen still hadn't returned. And he hadn't seen Allison since Stephen told her he had to go to work and she stomped off to a table to sit alone. Not the party she hoped for. He sent a text to Stephen to tell him the party had ended, but he didn't reply. Must be buried in the paperwork he mentioned.

"Hey there." Cori stood on the other side of the counter, no longer dressed in her costume.

He pocketed his phone. "Well, hey there, Mrs. Claus." He noticed her red shirt and leaned over the counter. Black capris and sandals. "Not Mrs. Claus."

Cori slid onto one of the barstools. "Allison and egg nog do not get along."

"Isn't she lactose intolerant?"

"It would seem so. I don't think she'll get her rental deposits back on either costume."

He grimaced. "Is she okay?"

"She's sleeping it off."

"Spiked too?"

"Yep."

Their banter hadn't changed, despite the years that had passed. Jeremy remembered loving that aspect of their relationship.

Several people walked by the kitchen, waving and thanking Jeremy for the great burgers and dogs before they left.

Cori watched them leave before turning back around. "Well done, Santa. You throw a great party."

"Yeah, not bad for a guy who only planned to stay for hors d'oeuvre."

"Parties still not your thing?" She did a half-smile and half-frown thing with her lips.

"Not really." He laughed. She remembered that about him?

"I know what you mean." She raised her brows as she popped a piece of cheese into her mouth. "I'm starved." She looked at the scraps left on the meat platter.

"I can fire the grill up again if you want a hot dog. I know there's more of those.

"No, don't bother. I'll eat at home." She scanned the area. "Is Stephen back yet?"

"No. And he isn't answering my text."

She gave him a concerned look. "Everyone's gone. I don't want to leave food while Allie's passed out."

"Tell you what, help me get the food put away and I'll reward you with dinner at this little place I know out on the beach."

She tilted her head in thought.

He really wanted her to say 'yes' and step back into the past, just a little, with the guy she used to call her best friend.

THEY CLEANED the place up in record time. Corinne was impressed by how well they worked together. She tackled the food table while he took care of collecting all the plates and cups.

Three giant garbage bags and an hour later, the place appeared back to normal. Aside from the explosion of Christmas decorations covering most of the house and a refrigerator maxed to the gills with leftovers. Allie could deal with all that later.

Since she didn't want to leave her car behind, she followed Jeremy to the place he mentioned. Some new place that just opened in the village. As she drove over the bridge onto Siesta Key, a slew of memories flooded her mind.

Hanging out with friends at the beach or the movies. Doing homework together—he helped her with math, she helped him with English. Then the graduation party—she'd shown up late and found Jeremy sitting by himself.

They blew off the party and went for a walk down the beach. Something had felt off about him that night, but he never opened up. So she chalked it up the realization that they'd soon be in different parts of the country for college.

A tap on the window brought her back to reality. Jeremy stood outside her door, smiling his familiar grin. How long has she sat here, lost in the past? She opened the door. "Sorry. Guess I have a lot on my mind."

His smile slid a bit. "Everything okay?"

"Yeah, I'm good. Just remembering the past a bit. I only moved back about a month ago and haven't had time to hit the beach yet."

He opened the door to the restaurant releasing a steady buzz of voices and the tantalizing aromas of grilled foods into the night. Her stomach jumped to full alert as she realized she'd eaten nothing at Allie's party.

"Wow, my mouth is already filling with saliva just from the smell."

Jeremy laughed.

She did a sudden intake of her breath. "Did I really say that? Is that TMI?"

"Not at all. You haven't changed much, Cori." The hostess led them to a booth near the back.

She slid in the far side so as the face the front of the restaurant—a habit she'd learned from going out with Peter. Best to have the exit scoped out in case he drank too much and started making a scene. She actually couldn't remember the last time she went out and relaxed at a restaurant.

And she had to admit, she breathed a sigh of relief when he ordered only iced tea when their server came to take their drink orders.

"Cori?"

"Oh, sorry. Lost in thought again." She grabbed the menu and mentally shook herself to stay in the present.

Jeremy set his menu aside. "I noticed Allison calls you by your full first name. Do you not use your nickname anymore?"

Dinner choice made, she set her menu on top of his. How did she answer that question without giving him information about her past that she'd rather not share? "Not really. I guess after college most people just called me Corinne and it stuck."

Why tell him that Peter didn't like her nickname and wanted her to use her full appropriate name. Nicknames were for children.

"Should I stop calling you Cori then?"

He stared at her with those gray-green eyes, as if he could see right into the very heart of her existence. Some things didn't change, or need to for that matter. "No, I like it when you call me Cori." She felt her cheeks heat up a bit and silently thanked the server for showing up with the water pitcher.

She always felt safe, like someone had her back when he gave her that slow smile.

Just like he did now...

CHAPTER 5

Once their food arrived, they spent most of the time catching up on career changes, moves, and miscellaneous details about their pasts. Cori seemed to avoid any discussion about her ex and which made it easy for Jeremy to avoid talking about his. He found himself more relaxed than he'd been out on a date in a long time.

But this wasn't a date... just friends reconnecting. Probably why he felt so at ease. Then again, he always did with Cori.

Toward the end of their meal, Corinne's cell chirped. She groaned and turned her phone over.

"Bad news?"

"Ugh, my mother. She, um," she put her hand out, "well, she hired a matchmaker."

Jeremy choked on his iced tea. "Did you say a matchmaker?"

"Yes, I did. She's determined to get me remarried as soon as possible."

After a swift recovery, he shook his head. "I can relate. My mother keeps trying to set me up on dates with women from her church."

"Seriously?" Her eyes widened, revealing the delicate sweep of her lashes.

"Yes. She invites me over for dinner and or asks me to take her to the store, but when I show up, she has a date waiting for me."

She gasped. "Wow, and I thought my mother was bad."

"Plus, my friends keep trying to set me up as well. Namely, your best friend."

"Allison?" She frowned.

"Yeah, but I think she finally learned her lesson when the last date went down in flames. Literally."

She squinted at him. "Flames? Do tell."

"Turns out when you combine a table candle and a polyester jacket with an amorous date who won't stay on her side of the table, you wind up with a clear disaster."

"Wow, was she hurt?"

"The jacket was mine."

"Oh!" She giggled. "Well, you seem okay."

"Yes, thank goodness suit jackets are thick."

She laughed again.

The sound created a warmth that spread across his chest. And he liked it. Maybe too much. He really didn't need to get involved with anyone right now. "It's so good to see you again, Cori."

As she smiled, a familiar twinkle settled into her eyes. He'd never been more thankful for the interruption of a cell phone.

She groaned.

"What's wrong?"

"It's my mother. She's sent a list of Christmas and New Years' events that she sent to the matchmaker." She held her head.

"Can't you say no?" He leaned back in the booth seat.

"Have you not met me?" She half laughed, half groaned as she put her phone on the table and waved her hands by her head. "When it comes to my mother, I go out of my way to make her happy. And these are all her country club events that I've missed through the years."

He drew his brows together. "And why is that? Didn't you and Peter visit at Christmas?"

She looked away before glancing down. "Long story."

What was she hiding about her past? He had a sense that things between her and Peter had been more difficult than she led on. As much as he preferred not to get involved with another person's mother drama, he felt a deep push to help Cori somehow.

Then an idea hit him. "Hey, I have an idea. What if you and I team up for any Christmas and New Year's events, that way we can tell our matchmaking mothers we already have dates."

She wrinkled her nose. "I don't know. What if they think we're a serious item or something?"

"Isn't that the idea?"

She shot him a questioning look.

He shook his head. "No, I mean, if they think we're serious, then they'll back off trying to fix us up. Once January comes, we can just say it didn't work out. That we make better friends than lovers." He didn't need the blush of Cori's cheeks to tell him he'd crossed over into the awkward zone. "Sorry, I didn't mean to imply anything."

She smiled with her nod. "It's okay." She shrugged. "Do you think it'll work?"

"Can't hurt to try, right?"

Another ding from her phone interrupted her hesitation. She read her screen. "The matchmaker already replied with three candidates!" She lifted desperate eyes to him. "Let's do it."

CORINNE CHECKED her outfit in the mirror and added her sparkly snowflake earrings to finish her holiday attire. Jeremy's semi-shocked expression when she listed the dates continued to haunt her though. He hadn't expected so many but reassured her it would be fine, seeing as he only had a two or three at the most. Still, she'd find a way to minimize her mother's excitement over having her home for the entire holiday.

Just as she left her bedroom, the doorbell rang. She snagged her clutch and the black shrug she'd chosen to complement her red dress. The Florida weather had finally transitioned to cooler temperatures, so she'd need a jacket for the evening. The thought reminded her of her days in California. And Peter. She pushed the memories aside and opened her door.

"Hey there!" He paused. "Wow, you look great." He did a quick scan of her attire before sticking his arms out. "Will this do?" He did a quick turn, giving her a full view of the tailored gray slacks and burgundy shirt beneath his tailored charcoal jacket.

She nodded her approval. "Definitely a step up from the jeans and T-shirts you wore in high school."

He brushed the gray at one side of his temples. "In case you haven't noticed, I've aged a bit."

She laughed as she closed her condo door. "Aged well, I'd say." She bit her lip as she realized what she said. Words had a way of escaping before she had a chance to consider them.

Jeremy's easy smile brought that twinkle back to his eyes. He seemed almost like the shy boy she first met in school. "I'm glad you approve. Now let's go show your mother what we're made of."

When they arrived, her mother's theater club party had already swung into full gear. Guests mingled in the front lobby of the theater and the adjoining wing that was part of a well-known art museum in the area. High-top tables speckled the rooms, their tops laden with bowls of Christmas hors d'oeuvres and sweets that surrounded a floral centerpiece composed of white poinsettias, glitter crusted branches, and sprigs of cedar.

She stopped at a table to touch a branch. Fresh pine filled her nose as she leaned in closer.

Jeremy popped a bacon-wrapped scallop into his mouth. "Quite a party."

"I should hope so." Her mother's voice came from behind them.

Corinne gave her mother a hug. "It's beautiful, Mom."

"Why thank you." Her eyes darted to Jeremy as she lifted her brows slightly.

"This is Jeremy Payne. Do you remember him, Mom?"

She held her hand out to Jeremy. "Margaret Carter. It's a pleasure to meet you again, Jeremy."

Jeremy gave her a slight nod of his head, almost a small bow. "Likewise, Mrs. Carter. I'm so glad Cori and I could reconnect."

Her mother smiled, yet the corners of her mouth remained tight, a telltale sign of her skepticism. "Might I borrow Corinne a moment, Jeremy?"

She didn't miss her mother's emphasis on her full name, and judging by the quick glance Jeremy gave her, he hadn't either.

"I'll be right back." She followed her mother as she headed to the other side of the room where a woman dressed in elegant Indian attire stood. "Mom, what are you doing?"

Her mother stopped and turned around. "I want you to meet the matchmaker."

"Why? I'm here with Jeremy. I don't need her to fix me up with anyone."

"Please, Corinne, it's the least you can do since she went to the trouble of suggesting suitable partners for you."

She tugged her mother's sleeve to stop her when she started to walk again. "I didn't hire her."

Her mother patted her hand. "Just do it for me, dear. Then I can explain you've decided to go another direction. Assuming this thing with Jeremy is for real?"

Had her mother somehow figured out she and Jeremy had an agreement? "What do you mean?"

Her mother tilted her head and stepped closer and rested her hand on her arm. "I mean serious. Heading somewhere. Have you two had that conversation yet?"

As much as she wanted to scream, she kept her voice to a rough whisper. "Mom, we just reconnected."

"Then you're not sure."

She had to scramble fast and make it believable. "Jeremy is kind and sweet. He was one of my best friends in high school and we still seem connected that way." She lowered her chin. "And he lets me be myself."

Her mother wrapped her in a hug. "Good, then just say hello and then you can get back to your date."

Corinne rolled her eyes but followed her mother. She could be a dutiful daughter for five minutes.

CHAPTER 6

Conversation with Cori was still as easy as Jeremy remembered. But an impulse hit him when he noticed a small band tucked in one of the alcoves of the lobby. Several couples of various ages danced to the upbeat music. The festivities of the evening heightened the expectation and excitement of Christmas. He took Cori's hand. "Let's dance."

"What?" She glanced over her shoulder. "Why?"

"Because you look amazing, and I need to work off some of these sweets."

She resisted at first, but then laughed and wound up reaching the dance area before he did. They laughed and shared memories of school dances and the antics of their teenaged friends.

The tempo of the music slowed from upbeat holiday tunes to *I'll Be Home for Christmas*. Twinkle lights dangled from the vaulted ceiling of the room and oversized snowflakes sparkled in-between. Slim silver Christmas trees framed the stage where the band played, giving the dance floor a winter wonderland feel.

Jeremy tugged Cori into his embrace for a slow dance. "Hope you don't mind a slow one."

She half laughed, half snickered. "Not at all. It's been quite a night."

He liked the way she felt in his arms. Though he was only a couple inches over six feet, with her heels, Cori's head almost reached to his nose and filled his senses with the heady scent of musk and vanilla. He closed his eyes and swayed with her.

"I'm not sure my mother's going to back off."

Her statement snapped him back to reality. He better stay on guard or he might wind up believing the lie himself. "She's only seen us together once. Just give her time." The music shifted back to an upbeat tempo. "In the meantime, we can just enjoy ourselves, eat some amazing and not so amazing food, and fall into bed exhausted."

Her surprised gaze connected with his as he twirled her out and then back to him.

"Separately!" He forced a laugh. Since when did words just pop out of his mouth? "You know what I mean."

No blush this time. Just a smile. "I know what you mean. And thank you."

"For what?"

"For not being that kind of guy."

The song ended. He squeezed her hand. "No problem."

JEREMY PULLED up in front of her condo building. "Thanks. You don't have to get out."

"I always walk my mother to her door." He got out of the car and met her on the sidewalk.

"Are you putting me in the same category as your mother?" Corrine kept her tone playful, matching the mood of their entire evening.

He gave her a mock expression of offense. "I would never do such a thing."

Their mutual laughter floated away on the crisp night air, leaving them in silence as they walked to her door.

She pulled out her keys. "I noticed my mother watching us several times."

"See? We'll have her convinced in no time." Jeremy pulled out his cell phone. "Just checking my calendar to see what the next event is."

She noticed his well-defined hands as he touched various squares on his virtual calendar and the scent of his cologne still lingered. Jeremy had definitely improved with age. And she could tell he worked out, keeping himself healthy and in good shape. She grabbed her wandering thoughts and smacked herself back into focus.

"...so I'll pick you up at seven."

Mind scrambling, she pieced together what she missed. Thankfully, she had most of the events in her memory. "Your mother's church party. Got it. Any special attire requirements"

He shook his head. "Nope. Just casual."

"Great. See you tomorrow."

He turned to head back to his car.

But she wanted to tell him something that had been on her mind all evening. "Jeremy."

As he turned around, the courtyard lamps silhouetted his figure, masking his face. "Yeah?"

She stepped away from her door. "Thank you for being a friend. I really need that right now. Means a lot."

He held his hands out from his sides for a moment. "No problem. You know me, always happy to help a friend in need."

The silence of the night fell between them again.

Best to leave it at that. She gave him a small wave. "Good night."

"Night." He waved back.

She let herself in the door but peeked out to make sure Jeremy got to his car. His headlights switched on as he drove away. She really did appreciate his friendship right now. And Jeremy was such a nice guy—honest and respectful. But so was Peter when they first dated and married.

Something in her gut told her to stay alert and guard her heart. She didn't need any complications in her life right now.

CHAPTER 7

The afternoon had turned out sunny, causing most to shed their jackets. Jeremy dropped his over the back of a folding chair near the table he and Corinne had claimed because of its proximity to the parking lot.

Meaning, once they did their obligatory nibble of a few of the dishes set up on the tables for the Christmas Potluck, they could be on their merry way.

Ho ho ho...

Jeremy didn't feel very festive. Hadn't since last night. He had no idea why Corinne's words of appreciation rubbed him the wrong way. Maybe it was his pride. He considered himself a decent catch, but he really didn't want to be caught at the moment. So, technically, he should be happy that she put him in the friend zone.

But he wasn't. He just hoped she hadn't seen his reaction last night. So far she seemed her usual self, though a bit quiet today. He pushed his musings aside and sat down.

"Jeremy?"

His mother's voice brought his head up. "Hi, Mom." He did his best to smile and appear happy as he stood and gave her a hug. But then his eyes fell on the woman standing a couple of feet behind her.

His mother beamed at him. "I have someone I want you to meet." She tugged the woman in front of her. "This is Sarah. She just moved here from Ohio."

Sarah glanced over her shoulder at his mother, looking as uncomfortable as he did. "Nice to meet you, Jeremy. Your mother has told me so much about you."

He didn't miss the emphasis on the 'so' and the unspoken message behind her words. This had to stop.

"Mom, I think it's time—"

"You met his old-new girlfriend." Cori stood next to him, her hand out to his mother. "Such a pleasure to meet you, Mrs. Payne."

From where she came, he had no idea. And he was more grateful than he could imagine a person feeling in a single moment.

His mother darted her gaze between them as Sarah tiptoed away. Looking quite relieved, from what he could tell. He'd have to find her later and apologize for his mother's "good" intentions.

"Jeremy told me you two reconnected. Funny thing is, I don't remember you two dating while he was in high school. Are you sure you two went out?" Her voice turned nasal as she spoke.

Cori put her arm around Jeremy's waist. "Probably because he played hard to get most of the year. Yet here we are years later, and I finally got him."

His mother's doubting expression shifted to pure delight. "Well, isn't that wonderful." She took Cori's hand and tugged her toward the buffet. "You must tell me everything, my dear. Jeremy can be quite a challenge, but you already know that."

Cori glanced back at him as his mother continued to prod her for details, but her smile never faltered.

If he hadn't suspected Cori was part angel, he most certainly did now.

SHE FLOPPED into the chair next to Jeremy. "Well, that was interesting." She'd made the rounds with Jeremy's mother as she introduced Corinne to several of her friends, even hinting at a future engagement. She had to bite her lip several times to keep her guilty conscience from clearing the record.

He swallowed his bite of food. "I was beginning to think she'd fixed you up with someone else."

When she noticed his mother was watching them, she leaned in closer to appear as if she were hugging Jeremy.

He stiffened at first.

"Your mother is watching us." She kept her lips near his ear so as not to be overheard. "And she pretty much hinted to everyone here that we're almost engaged."

He tucked his head into the nape of her neck, sending a shiver down her back with his breath as he laughed softly. "You know how to play your part well."

She gently pushed him away. "I feel awful about it."

"Why?" His signature smile spread across his face.

"Don't look so pleased. Your poor mother. She's going to be devastated when we *break* it off."

"But she'll be happy as a lark until then."

She scanned the crowd by the food tables. His mother smiled and gave her a quick wave. She groaned. "I don't know, Jeremy."

He intertwined his fingers with hers and kissed the back of her hand.

"Stop it!" She whispered but put some force behind her voice. "You're just making it worse."

"All right. Sorry. You just have no idea how many women my mother has tried to set me up with. You saw her in action. Poor Sarah. I think she left as soon as she had a chance."

Corinne giggled. "Okay, when you put it in that light..."

He stared into her eyes, giving her a sense of the mischief to come. Then she remembered what a prankster he was in school.

She forced a warning tone in her voice. "Jeremy, what are you up to?"

He slipped to one knee. "Corinne Carter, will you marry me?"

CHAPTER 8

His mother's squeal brought every set of eyes their way. Jeremy still held her hand as he mouthed, *I'm sorry*.

With a fixed smile, she squeezed his hand until her fingernails dug into his hand and mouthed back, *do something!*

He put his arm around her shoulder as his mother bounced closer, hands holding her cheeks.

She grabbed Corinne's hands. "Did you answer him?" She bounced her gaze to Jeremy. "What did she say?" Then back to Corinne. "Oh, please say yes? Jeremy will make a great husband. And father."

Since they were technically at a church, she prayed a silent prayer for God to snatch her up now. Or give her some way out of this disaster.

"I, uh, well—"

"Mom, I was just kidding. Do you think I'd spring a question like that in front of a crowd of people?"

At her crestfallen expression, he took his mother's hands in his, leaning his head down so she would look at him. "I'm so sorry I created a commotion."

His mother's smile spread, slow and easy like her son's. "I know I put a lot of pressure on you." She kissed his cheek.

"Yes, you do. So can we agree to leave my love life off the table? I'd really appreciate it."

"For now." She glanced at Corinne. "I agree to back off until you two figure things out."

Corinne breathed a sigh of relief. His mother didn't hate her. Or, more importantly, her son. And she had to admit, her admiration meter for Jeremy went up a few notches. He didn't make up a story. He was honest. And in a loving way.

His mother took her hand. "I'm sorry if my reaction put any pressure on you, my dear. You just seem so much better suited to my Jeremy than his previous fiancée."

Fiancée? Jeremy never mentioned being engaged before. Come to think of it, he hadn't said much about his previous relationships. But neither had she. "No worries, Mrs. Payne."

"Please call me Elizabeth. Or Liz. Most people call me Liz." She let out a nervous laugh.

"All right, Liz it is."

As his mother waddled off with some of her friends, Corinne faced Jeremy but remained silent. She really didn't know what to say.

He gave her a sad smile. "I'll take you home now."

"That would be great." She waited for him to grab his jacket after he helped her put on hers.

They walked to the car in silence. When he opened the passenger door, she turned around. "I know that was a semi disaster back there—"

He put his hand up. "I know, my bad. And I am so sorry. If you want to scrap this idea, I totally understand."

She paused long enough to consider his suggestion and her words. "No, let's keep our agreement. But I wanted to say, I love how honest you were with your mother. And kind."

His smile returned with a hint of awkwardness. "Thanks."

"And now I get why you suggested we do this. She's determined."

"No kidding."

She waited for Jeremy to get in the car. "So, you were engaged before?"

He started the engine but didn't move the car. "No."

"Weren't interested in marriage?"

He backed out of the parking space. "No, she wasn't."

Jeremy seemed closed mouth about it so she didn't ask any more questions, which would open up the discussion of their exes. And that was one topic she preferred not to visit.

THE FOLLOWING FRIDAY, they attended Jeremy's work party. Cori was an instant hit, and he didn't miss some of the admiring looks he received, which he promptly ignored. He wasn't interested in making up details of his pretend love life, so best to just avoid the conversation altogether.

On Sunday, they attended a banquet at her mother's polo club. Jeremy didn't even know Sarasota had a polo club and found the festivities quite entertaining, watching the riders swing their mallets, the horses romp at top speeds, and the overall excitement of the competition.

That is until he spotted Sheridan. The riders had taken a break and several surrounded her in what appeared to be an admiration club. Typical Sheridan. She loved being the center of attention and clearly, she knew she held the reins in that group.

He turned around to find Cori. The last thing he wanted was to see his ex, although the idea of making her think he'd moved on and was with Cori now had its appeal. But for some reason, it felt disrespectful. Especially to Cori, which made no sense.

Jeremy spotted her by one of the horses. The rider had made himself available for questions. As Jeremy walked over, the man helped lift Cori into the saddle and seemed very attentive, which also seemed to irritate Jeremy. Seeing Sheridan had to be messing with him.

He shielded his eyes as he looked up. "Hi."

She smiled down at him while stroking the horse's neck. "Hey there. Isn't he beautiful?"

"Yes, quite." He cleared his throat. "I'm not feeling great. Would you mind if we left?"

Concern creased her brows as she slid off the horse. Again, with help from the rider, who seemed much too attentive. "Are you okay?"

"Yeah, just something I ate, I'm sure."

"Okay, sure." She turned and thanked the player before joining him in the walk to the car. They were about twenty feet away from the parking lot when Sheridan's familiar voice called out his name.

He turned around. "Sheridan." He kept his tone light as he greeted her with a kiss on the cheek. "I didn't expect to see you here. I thought you were in Italy with your parents for the holidays."

The short white dress Sheridan wore accented her curves perfectly, as usual. Red heels were her only splash of color. The woman always found a way to make a statement.

She smiled but darted a questioning look at Cori, who stood a couple of feet behind him still. "I decided to stay stateside this year."

He nodded, then gestured to Cori. "This is Corinne Carter, a dear friend."

Sheridan extended her hand. "Nice to meet you, Corinne."

"Nice to meet you too."

"I hope you two aren't leaving already. The best part is yet to come." Sheridan darted her gaze back and forth between them.

"Jeremy said he wasn't feeling great." Cori gave him a quick smile of concern.

"Oh, of course, best to get some rest." Sheridan pinned him with her dark eyes, outlined heavenly in black, to give her a more sultry look. He knew that because she'd practiced it for hours in front of a mirror. "I do hope I see you again, Jeremy."

He didn't say a word. Just nodded and waved as he returned to his route to the parking lot. Thankfully, Cori didn't ask questions as they hoofed it to the car.

Once inside, he exhaled his relief.

"So, that was Sheridan." Cori watched him, but he didn't meet her eyes. "She seems intense."

"That's one way to describe her."

CHAPTER 9

Corinne couldn't shake the feeling that something big had gone down between Jeremy and Sheridan. His mood seemed downcast the entire trip home, and he didn't argue with her when she said she could walk herself to her door. Even though it was still daylight, Jeremy always insisted on accompanying her.

She'd texted him later that evening to see how he was feeling. He answered with one word—'fine.' She figured he was anything but *fine*. If Peter had appeared at an event, she would have had totally tanked.

All day at work, Jeremy stayed on her mind. She questioned her concern, but then realized, like Jeremy, she had a tender place for a friend in need. And Jeremy Payne was in need.

She left work early and stopped to grab the food she'd ordered before heading to Jeremy's place. She knew his address but had yet to see where he lived as he always came to pick her up for their fake dates.

He owned a small house on a side street off one of the older, quainter streets near downtown. She remembered the area growing up when she and her family made a trek to the beach but hadn't been back in years. The area still held the same quaint Florida neighborhood feel, with nearly flat rooflines and rocks in the flower beds.

She parked on the street and studied his mid-century modern-looking house. Suited him to a T. She grabbed the food bag and headed to his front door.

He answered the bell dressed in a pair of loose-knit shorts and a T-shirt. "Corinne?" He checked his watch. "Did I forget a date?"

"No, I just thought you could use a friend right now." She held up the bag. "And some dinner."

He studied her for a moment. Then his easy smile showed up, bringing some light back to his gray-green eyes. "Yeah, come in. Sounds great."

The first thing she noticed was the lack of clutter and the low-profile furniture. Very simple and practical. Much like Jeremy. She set the bag on the round dining room table. Black leather sling chairs surrounded it.

She shrugged off her jacket. "Nice place. Suits you."

He took her coat and hung it on the back of a chair. "Thanks. I love the Mid-Century Modern style that Sarasota is known for."

"It was pretty common in California, too. More European but very similar."

He took a container out of the bag and sniffed. "Lobster bisque?" He tilted the bag to look at the restaurant logo. "One of my favorites."

"Mine too. And lobster bisque is fancy comfort food."

He chuckled. "I agree. Thanks."

They sat at his high-top counter, eating the soup with the crusty bread included. Corinne didn't bother to pull the salads out. No reason to rush their meal. And she sensed he needed time to adjust to her presence in his home.

She set her spoon in the empty styrofoam container and sat back. "Care to talk about it?"

He pushed aside his bowl and wiped his mouth. "Not particularly, but I guess I owe you an explanation."

She shrugged. "You don't owe me anything, Jeremy. This isn't real, remember?"

"I know, but we're friends and friends share their lives, right?"

She glanced down. Did she want to share the details of her life with Peter? As she thought about it, for the first time she felt she actually could. "Yes, definitely friends. Close friends, like you told Sheridan."

He snickered. "Yes, figured honesty was best."

"I'm glad you did." She reached into the bag and pulled out their salads. "So eat your veggies and talk. Honestly."

THEY'D FINISHED their salads and moved on to the roasted portabella mushroom sandwich she'd chosen for them to share. The funk from seeing Sheridan had lifted considerably, thanks to Cori. Made him realize how much he'd internalized his breakup.

"Good thing I love mushrooms. Not everyone does." He took a generous bite of his half, enjoying the combination of grilled portabella and roasted red pepper.

"True, but I remembered that you loved mushrooms, so I knew it was a safe bet."

Sandwich poised for another bite, Jeremy paused. "You remember that?"

Cori finished chewing and swallowed. "Yeah, I do. And some other stuff."

"Like what?" He wiped his mouth with the napkin and set the rest of his sandwich down. What he remembered most about their friendship was how at ease, connected, and understood he always felt when he was with her... like he did now.

She looked up as she tried to remember. "Mr. Barrett's English class. Final project. You did a rap song about the Renaissance era."

He groaned. "Now why would you remember that?"

She giggled behind her hand. "How could I forget it? The expression on Mr. Barrett's face was enough to ingrain the memory alone. I'd never seen him so offended."

Jeremy laughed. "Yeah, I remember that. He thought I'd insulted all the great Renaissance artists with my musical garbage."

She gasped. "He did not call it garbage, did he?"

"Yeah, he did. He said I insulted what the era stood for—innovative excellence."

"What did you say?"

"As I recall, I told him that my idea was innovative and original and that the Renaissance artists were criticized and underappreciated for their work too."

"Wow…"

"Yeah, he didn't agree."

She laughed again. "I can only imagine."

"What else do you remember?" He dug into the rest of his sandwich as she thought.

"Oh, remember the beach party?"

The memories of that night rushed in like a tidal wave. "Yeah, I remember. We wound up walking down the beach and talking the rest of the night. I kinda felt bad about that actually."

"Why?"

"Because I took you away from the party."

She shrugged. "Eh, it wasn't that fun to begin with. Our walk was the best part."

He studied her as she cleaned up the remnants of their dinner. "Let's do it again."

She stopped to look at him. "Do what?"

"Go for a walk. On the beach."

She glanced down at her slacks and heels. "I'm not exactly dressed for that." She glanced at her watch. "And by the time I ran home, it would be too dark."

"I have a pair of sweatpants you can borrow, and bare feet are best for the beach."

"That's very true. I just have one question."

"Shoot."

She donned a playful expression. "Are the sweatpants clean?"

CHAPTER 10

The sun made a slow descent toward the ocean, releasing an explosion of red, orange, and yellow into the sky. Waves lapped the sand gently, nudged forward from a blue iridescent sea. Corinne inhaled deeply, then sighed as she exhaled.

"I know, right?" Jeremy smiled at her. "It's life-giving out here."

She nodded. "I should have done this sooner."

They walked in silence for a while, taking in the changing sky and fellow beachcombers. She tugged the hoodie Jeremy had loaned her tighter around her neck. Though the evening wasn't as cold as she'd grown accustomed to in California this time of year, the night air still held a chill.

"Thanks for the loaner." She tugged at the band of the sweatpants. "I'll try to forget they belonged to your ex."

He snorted. "Just hadn't had a chance to send them back to her. She'd probably tell me to donate the whole box at this point."

She dared to delve a little deeper, knowing she'd more than likely have to answer a few questions of his. "When did you guys break up?"

"About a year ago. But that was just the official breakup." He made air quotes. "At first it was hard. But then I realized we'd really stopped being a couple quite a while before that."

"What happened?"

"People change, I guess. Sheridan wanted a life that was much more 'visible.' I didn't."

"She and my mother would get along great."

He laughed with her before the silence returned.

"Cori, can I ask what happened with you and Peter. You two were together a long time."

She sighed. "Yeah, we were. But it was kind of the same thing as you and Sheridan. We wanted different things. Took a few years for us to realize we'd be better off apart." She paused. "That's the hard part, isn't it?"

"What is?" She didn't feel ready to talk about Peter's drinking and hoped Jeremy wouldn't delve deeper.

"Letting go of what's familiar."

"I suppose."

The silence returned as the sunset faded. They turned around and headed back to the small path that ran between the northern part of Siesta Key Beach and a small parking lot.

"I'm really glad you moved back, Cori."

She stopped. "Yeah, I am too. I was trying to remember why we didn't stay in touch."

"I remember. You started dating Peter during your first semester."

She tilted her head back. "Yeah, I guess I was a little obsessed with him. I'm sorry I didn't stay in touch. I regret that."

He tucked a piece of hair that had escaped her ponytail behind her ear. His fingers felt warm, like his gaze which trailed a path from her eyes to her lips. "There's something I regret too."

Her mind told her to back off, step back—do something to put distance between them, but her heart had a different desire.

To feel wanted again…loved. But could she risk her heart like that again?

As he moved closer, she felt his heart beating against her palm. She lifted her head to meet his kiss. Only one way to find out.

❋

THE MOMENT THEY STOPPED WALKING, he knew he was in trouble. Memories weren't the only thing flooding back. The way he felt about Cori all those years ago made a subtle appearance at first and then shifted into something new. And stronger.

He moved closer. Her skin felt icy from the breeze and made him want to pull her into his arms. He lowered his head.

Jeremy kept the kiss light at first to gauge her reaction, so when she leaned into his embrace, he deepened it. Every part of him focused on the taste, touch, and smell of her. Even the silkiness of her hair as her ponytail brushed his hand. He lifted his head before he completely lost his senses.

A series of emotions fluttered across her face. Wonder, confusion, then concern. "I didn't realize you felt that way back then."

"I didn't know how to tell you."

She dropped her gaze. "And now?"

He lifted her chin. "I've never been great with words." He captured her lips again and allowed his emotions to speak through the kiss.

The sound of whispers broke their kiss. Two teenage girls walked up the path to where they stood, full of shy smiles and giggles as they glanced at them.

Jeremy kept his forehead against Cori's head until they passed by. He took Cori's hand and walked to the car. They didn't talk during the short ride back to his house. And Cori didn't seem to mind him holding her hand the entire way back.

After he pulled into the driveway, he cut the engine and let the silence settle into the car. He wanted to ask Cori what she was thinking. What she was feeling...

She turned in the seat to face him. "I don't know what this is, but I don't want to rush into anything, Jeremy." She intertwined her fingers with his.

Did she regret their kisses? Should he have stayed in the friend zone?

"But I think I'd like to date you. For real. If you're interested?" She tilted her head and smiled at him.

He chuckled. "I'm very interested."

CHAPTER 11

The restaurant buzzed with a decent lunch crowd. Corinne studied her menu as she waited for Allison to arrive. Her last text said she was running a few minutes late, but that had to be a good five minutes ago. She set the menu down and checked the front entrance again.

Allison stood near the hostess stand, scanning the place.

Corinne waved at her.

"So sorry." Allison sat as she dumped her purse into the chair between them.

"Everything okay?"

"Yes, just had to run something up to Stephen at his office. He left a client file at the house."

She studied her friend for some indication of how things stood with her and Stephen. Allison hadn't brought up the whole Christmas party disaster, and Corinne didn't want to make her friend uncomfortable bringing it up. "Okay."

Allie stared at her. "What?"

Corinne raised her shoulders. "Nothing. Just concerned about you two."

"We're fine." Allie leaned forward. "Just my imagination going a little crazy. Stephen apologized when he got home. He thought one of the interns had wired a transfer, but apparently dropped the ball instead. They almost lost a major account."

"Wow."

"Yeah, no kidding." Allie studied the menu in front of her. "And thank you, by the way."

"For what?"

"Taking care of things." She put her menu down. "I'm sorry I did that to you."

"What? Puke all over my Mrs. Santa costume?"

Allie groaned. "I did puke, didn't I?"

"Yes, you did." She laughed.

"And left you and Jeremy to clean up, I hear. I'm so sorry."

Corinne fiddled with her menu. "It worked out okay."

Allison smacked the table. "You two hit it off, didn't you?"

"Allie, we used to be good friends. Best friends."

"That was then. So what's going on now?"

She couldn't hold back her grin. "I don't know. Maybe something."

Their server came with water and took their orders.

Allie leaned back in her seat. "Jeremy's a great guy, but are you sure you want to step into a relationship right now?"

"It's not really a relationship yet. We're just getting reacquainted. And helping each other avoid our mothers' attempts to play matchmaker."

"Both of them?"

Corinne rolled her eyes. "My mother actually hired a matchmaker."

"No way!"

"And Jeremy's mother isn't much better. I went with him to a Christmas Potluck at her church. The woman greeted him with a woman in tow."

Allie choked on her sip of water. "Wow. Poor Jeremy. Now I understand why he was so resistant to my attempts to fix him up."

"Yeah, I heard about that. Something about burning polyester, right?" She let a little sarcasm into her tone. Why did she feel the need to protect Jeremy?

"He told you about that?" Allie covered her eyes with her hand. "I still feel awful about that." She dropped her hand into her lap. "He knows that, right? I told Stephen to tell him."

"Yes, he knows."

"Good."

She had the sudden realization that they spoke about him as if she and Jeremy had been together a long time. Made things feel more intimate than they were. She took a deep breath and gulped down some of her water.

The server came with their lunch orders and set them on the table. Corinne picked up her fork, grateful for the distraction.

Allie reached out and touched her wrist. "I don't know the full story behind you and Peter, but I'm happy to see you moving on, Corinne."

"Yeah, me too." She busied herself with food, hoping the butterfly stampede in her stomach was due to hunger and not nerves.

With her thoughts consumed with Jeremy's kiss and what it could mean, she'd slept very little through the night. Some of what she felt reminded her of the first dates she had with Peter. Everything felt good and exciting. Yet their marriage had begun to fail not long after their nuptials were said and his true personality came out.

But Jeremy seemed... different. Real and honest. Just like she remembered him in high school.

"Corinne?"

She blinked. "Yeah?"

"Did you hear what I said?"

"No, sorry."

Allie pointed with her fork. "That guy over there. He reminds me of Peter."

Corinne swiveled in her seat to look behind her. The butterflies in her stomach crashed and burned. 'That's because it is."

THE DRIVE HOME from work confirmed that Christmas shoppers were out in full swing with just days to finish their shopping. Took him a good fifty percent longer to get home than normal. But he didn't mind that much. Gave him more time to think about Cori. They'd gone out to dinner or walked the beach almost every evening the last week. No events required.

The Christmas Eve Gala Ball at her mother's country club was in three days. He'd already rented a tux and spent a fair bit on a new pair of shoes in anticipation of twirling her on the dance floor. Saturday couldn't get here fast enough.

As he pulled into his driveway, he noted the cute sports coupe parked in front of his house. Bright candy apple red. Made him think of Sheridan. A closer look confirmed it was the Miata she'd always wanted. But the car was empty…

He let himself in through the garage, set his satchel on the dining room table, and headed into the living room.

And there she sat, legs crossed, wearing a stunning red dress to match her car, and a smile on her face that meant she had an agenda.

He walked a few steps closer but kept his distance. "Sheridan, what are you doing here?"

She lifted her hand. A key dangled from her finger. "I still had your key. Hope you don't mind."

Tension built between his shoulder blades. He did a quick stretch back and forth with his head to release the muscles in his neck. "I do actually." He held his hand out.

She uncrossed her legs and stood in one graceful motion. "Sorry. I didn't mean to offend." Pouting, she placed the key in his hand, along with another one, then smiled again. "I thought you might like to drive my new toy."

Her perfume filled his nostrils, along with the musky scent he'd grown familiar with. He felt the longing in his body but didn't want familiar anymore. He wanted something new. Something fresh and honest. Someone like Cori.

He shook his head and went to the front door, pulling it open. "No thanks, Sheridan. I think it best you leave."

She sighed as she grabbed her purse from the couch. "I thought you'd be happy to see me, Jeremy."

"Why? You're the one who said you weren't happy, that you wanted more fun and excitement." His residual anger made his voice sound rougher than he intended.

Her eyes turned glassy. "I was wrong. I miss you."

Jeremy swallowed the lump in his throat. He wasn't heartless, but he could not let her tactics manipulate him anymore. "You and I both know that you're just feeling that way because it's Christmas. You usually do this time of year because you miss your parents."

"See? You know me so well. I love that."

"Obviously not enough to marry me when I asked you."

A lone tear slipped down her cheek. "I should have said yes."

He didn't want her to leave feeling hurt, but she was better off with the truth so she could move on. "It's for the best, Sheridan. You and I wanted different things. And, well, I've started dating Cori now."

She pursed her lips and pulled her shoulders back. A clear sign of her anger. "I thought you were just friends."

"We were but now we're more."

She nodded her head and gave him a pale smile. "Well then, I wish you two the best."

"Thank you."

She leaned in and kissed him on the cheek as a car passed by then rushed out to her car.

He waited for her to pull away and then went back into his house, feeling lighter than he had in months. As much as he didn't like Sheridan just showing up like that, maybe he needed it. Now he had some closure. And a release from trying to figure out what went wrong with their relationship. Now he knew without a doubt they were just too different.

CHAPTER 12

The coffee shop had seemed a safe place to sit and talk with Peter, but no matter how hard she tried, Corinne could not get comfortable sitting across from the man who'd basically wrecked her life during the last five years of their marriage.

Once he sat down at the table, she let her guns rip. "What are you doing here, Peter?"

He wore his hair shorter than normal, almost a buzz cut. And his eyes and skin looked bright and healthy. Not the usual dull and waxy look from the alcohol. "I wanted to share my good news with you, Corinne. I'm finally sober."

"You've said that before."

He bobbed his head in agreement. "I know, but it's different this time."

"You've said that before too." Her entire body stiffened with the pain and anger she still held. She leaned forward. "It's too late, Peter. I trusted you over and over again, tried to help you, but you just walked all over me. Didn't care about how you ruined my life. I even lost my job because of you."

"I know, and I'm so sorry. And that's the reason I'm here. To make amends." He reached out and touched her hand holding her coffee cup. "I know I screwed up big time, Cori. I know I ruined your life and didn't appreciate what you sacrificed to help me regain mine. But I'm sober now, going on almost a year now."

He called her Cori... he never liked using her nickname. Life with Peter was always about him, his preferences. Was he just using a tactic on her?

She pulled her hand away. "What do you want, Peter?"

He glanced down at his empty hand. "I came to ask you for your forgiveness. That's how these programs work."

She shot her gaze to meet his and saw nothing deceitful in his brown eyes. He didn't look away or blink rapidly—things she'd learned to identify when he lied to her. "You stayed in a program?"

"Yes, that's the only way I could get sober and stay clean. I finally listened. And I'm so glad I did." He smiled at her—the warm smile he remembered from when she met him in college. Maybe he really had changed.

"So will you forgive me, Cori?"

"You never used to like to call me that."

"I know, and I'm sorry for being a jerk about that. I guess I felt like I had to compete with that guy you were friends with back then."

She frowned. "You mean Jeremy?"

"Yeah."

"I never knew that. Why would you think you had to compete? We were just friends, Jeremy and me."

He shrugged. "I know that now. I was just insecure. That's what the drinking was always about. Insecurity. I know that now and I know how to deal with it. I've come a long way." He reached out and raised his brows in question. "I hope you can forgive me."

She hesitated at first, then put her hand in his. "I'd like to. I want to."

He broke into a wide smile. "Good! Thank you." He squeezed her hand and let go. "I can't step into a relationship with someone else until I have things settled between us. It's part of my healing process."

Someone else? He didn't want to get back together with her. He just wanted to clear his guilty conscience. "Is that what this is about? I thought you were trying to get back together?"

His shocked expression gave her little comfort. "Oh, Cori, I'm sorry. I didn't mean... I never intended..." He cleared his throat. "I, uh, I met someone. About three months ago. She's been a major force in helping me get clean, but I didn't feel right about taking our relationship further until I settled things with you."

Corinne nodded. Accepted yet another failure on her part. She'd clearly not been enough or done enough to help Peter stay sober. "I see."

Peter looked lost. "And now I've hurt you. And I'm sorry for that. But now we can both move on and live healthy lives. You helped me see that too. When you left, I had no one to lean, no one to make decisions for me anymore. I had to choose for myself."

She didn't bother to wipe the tears tumbling down her cheeks. She didn't care if anyone noticed. And she didn't care if her waterworks made Peter uncomfortable.

She rose from the table. "Have a nice life, Peter. I hope everything works out for you."

Once inside her car, she let the full range of her emotions go. She threw her purse down and pounded on the steering wheel, then sobbed some more.

But why? Why was she really upset? Deep down she knew she didn't love Peter anymore. She'd been so young when they married she doubted she even understood what true love was. Lasting love. Not a love that enabled or covered for someone's sickness.

So why was she upset? She dried her face with a napkin she found in her glove box and drove. She needed to talk to someone.

She checked her watch. Allie would still be at Stephen's company Christmas party. Her mother was definitely not an option. Maybe this was a good time to open up and talk to Jeremy? About Peter and what happened between them.

When the light turned green, she did a U-turn and headed to Jeremy's place. She'd suggest a walk on the beach and just be honest with him.

As she drove down the street and neared his house, she spotted a red sports car parked in front. At the front door, she recognized Jeremy, then Sheridan, as she went up on tiptoe to kiss him.

Corinne didn't slow down. Just kept going until she came to the end of the street and then turned to head home.

Alone, which seemed to be her fate these days.

Once home, she sent Jeremy a text, canceling their date for the ball. Might as well cut things off as soon as possible. Better for her and better for him if he's seeing Sheridan again.

Her tears threatened to make a reappearance. She sure knew how to pick them, didn't she? Peter loved the bottle more than her, and now Jeremy chose his ex over her. And she'd really thought they could have a great relationship. She'd even let herself imagine what a big picture could look like with him. They said best friends made the best and lasting relationships, but what made her think Jeremy wanted that too? Maybe she was just a placeholder for him.

Inside her condo, she tossed her purse onto a chair and kicked off her shoes with a grunt. She was tired of letting fate run her life. Maybe her mother was right. Maybe she did need someone to help her find the right person to spend her life with—someone who didn't have addiction issues or exes hanging around. Maybe she needed help finding someone willing to love her for herself.

Peter said he made a choice to get sober. And she knew her choice to forgive him was the right one, even if her feelings didn't line up with it yet. In time, her resentment and anger would fade as she healed.

But it was high time she'd make a choice for herself. She picked up her cell and called her mother.

"Hello, Corinne. How are you?"

How was she? "I'm actually very clear-headed at the moment, Mom."

Her mother laughed. "Well, that's good, dear."

"Yes, yes it is. Which is why I'm calling. Can you contact the matchmaker and tell her I'd like to consider some of her candidates, specifically for the ball."

"Are you sure? I thought you and Jeremy were dating."

"Yeah, that didn't work out."

"All right then. I'll call her right now."

❋

As he waited for Stephen to join him for their usual workday lunch, Jeremy read Cori's text again.

Not going to the Christmas ball, so you're off the hook.

And she still hadn't replied to his reply, asking why. He had the tux, the shoes, and a plan in mind to show Cori he really cared about her. But now, she seemed to be blowing him off.

No, she was acting like she was scared. Something happened to set her off. But what?

Stephen strode out the door of his building and joined him on the sidewalk. "The usual?"

"Sounds good." Jeremy punched the crosswalk button. "Hey, has Allison said anything to you about Cori?"

"Like what?"

"Like why she blew me off for the Christmas Eve Ball."

"Did you ask her yourself?"

"Allison?"

"No, Cori."

They waited for the next crosswalk light to change.

"Yeah, she won't reply and she didn't answer my call."

"Then I'm guessing it's because she thinks you're back with Sheridan."

"I'm what? That's not true."

"Hey man, no judgment here. All I know is Cori told Allison she saw you kissing Sheridan." Stephen stepped up to the food truck window to place his order.

Jeremy's only encounter with Sheridan had been at his house that day. Then it hit him. The car going too fast must have been Cori. He groaned. "She saw Sheridan kissing me."

"Same thing, buddy."

"No, it wasn't. I got home from work, and Sheridan was waiting for me. She wanted to get back together, but I told her she did me a favor. We weren't right for each other. I also told her I was dating Cori. Sheridan kissed me on the cheek to say goodbye."

Stephen held his hands out to his sides. "All I know is Cori thinks you dumped her for Sheridan, so she's trying things her mother's way."

"You mean the matchmaker?" He growled. "You've got to be kidding."

"Nope, sorry to tell you, she already has a date for the ball too."

CHAPTER 13

Corinne didn't expect to be picked up in a limo, but Samuel seemed intent on making a lasting impression upon her tonight. They'd met briefly the day before for coffee, at the behest of the matchmaker, to see if they were at all compatible.

After a few minutes of awkwardness, they'd fallen into a conversation about their professions and interests. And when she mentioned the Christmas Eve Ball, Samuel said he'd love to take her, so she'd said yes. Why waste the dress and shoes she'd purchased just for the occasion?

Now he'd opened her door and stood waiting for her to take his hand. As she put one foot out, the overhead street lamp made her gold shoes sparkle and reflected the emerald green of her full-length gown. She laid her hand on his arm when he offered it and allowed him to lead her up the stairs leading to the country club entrance.

She spotted her mother standing by one of the entrances and pointed in that direction to let Samuel know.

"Mother, how wonderful you look." She leaned over to kiss her mother's cheek and then admired the shimmer of the short brocade jacket she wore over a straight line black dress.

"Thank you, dear." She appraised Corinne's date. "So this must be Samuel." She held out her hand.

Samuel took her hand but didn't shake it. "Yes, a pleasure to meet you, Mrs. Carter."

Her mother raised her brow in approval at Corinne.

She tugged Samuel toward the entry before her mother could cross-examine him. "We'll talk to you later, Mother."

Once inside, she allowed herself a few moments to take in all the Christmas decorations and arrangements. The standard chandeliers glowed at a softer level, giving the crystals a warm glow. Glass teardrop-shaped jars filled with twinkling fairy lights hung in-between them. Life-size Nutcrackers stood on both sides of a doorway swagged with a pine garland decorated with sparkling green ribbon and red Christmas balls.

They passed into the main hall, which was awash in twinkling lights strung across the room with dangling snowflakes. On the stage, a stack of oversized gifts sat on one side and a cluster of giant Christmas balls on the other. Tables of food lined both ends of the room with intimate clusters of tables seating two or four people. The overall effect was breathtaking.

She gasped. "Wow..."

"I agree." Samuel stared at her with appreciation.

He nodded toward the dance floor, where at least twenty-five to thirty couples danced to a Christmas waltz. "Shall we?"

"Yes, please."

They danced through one song with some light conversation. The second song sent several couples off the floor with its fast-paced beat, but Samuel seemed fine with the tempo. She laughed as they danced to another song.

The evening was turning out better than she hoped. Maybe this matchmaker thing could really work out for her. If she could stop thinking about Jeremy... she'd glanced at the main doors more than once to see if he'd on his own, but afraid she'd see him with Sheridan draped on his arm.

Samuel twirled her away from him, but another set of arms caught her.

"Jeremy." She said his name in a breathy whisper.

"Cori." He slid his arm around her waist, took her other hand in his, and then nodded at Samuel as he moved in the other direction. "I'm cutting in."

Corinne tried to follow where Samuel stood, but Jeremy kept moving in circles. "Stop it. You're being rude."

He gave a short laugh. "I'm being rude? You're the one who wouldn't answer my calls or texts."

"I didn't see any point. I already knew what you were going to say." She tried not to look into his eyes, but couldn't help herself. No one looked at her that way. Not even Samuel's appraisal made her feel like Jeremy did when he looked at her that way. Like she mattered more than anything in the world.

"And that was?"

She dragged her gaze to the side. "That you and Sheridan were back together."

"Because you saw her kiss me."

"Yes."

"Yeah, I had to find that out from Stephen. Why didn't you stop and ask me what was going on, Cori? Don't you care about me at all?"

She snapped her eyes back to his. "Care? What makes you think I don't care about you? I do care, but I can't compete with Sheridan and have no desire to."

"Sheridan and I are not back together." He pulled her closer for emphasis. "Yes, she wanted to get back together, but I told her I was seeing you now. What you saw was her saying goodbye."

CORINNE SEEMED to settle in against him. Did that mean she believed him? He'd maneuvered them to a more isolated part of the dance floor to give them some privacy.

He led them off the floor and held her hands. "Cori, being with you made me realize how much I missed you. Not just as a friend... but more. A lot more."

Her eyes darted back and forth as she searched his face. "Me too."

She still seemed hesitant, but he didn't know what else he could say to convince her. He tugged her against him and kissed her with all the emotion he could pour into one kiss.

At first, she responded, but then she pushed him away. "I'm sorry. This just won't work." She ran across the dance floor past her date, who ran after her out of the building.

Jeremy headed in the same direction, maneuvering around the dance floor to catch her before she was gone for good.

Corrine's mother stopped him in the lobby. "She already left. Jeremy, what did you say to make her so upset."

He ran a hand through his hair. "Only that I cared about her and that I wanted more." He turned away from Margaret, then spun around again. "I'm falling in love with your daughter, but I can't seem to convince her I mean it."

Margaret waved her hand in front of her nose. "Let me ask you something. Did you have a drink at the bar?"

"Yes, a little champagne. Not something I usually do but I needed a little courage."

"Peter was an alcoholic."

He swallowed. "She never told me that."

She lifted one shoulder. "She never told me either, but I knew. Even three thousand miles couldn't hide what was obvious."

He covered his mouth with his hand for a moment. "When I kissed her…"

"Corrine is still healing, Jeremy. She wound up back here because she wanted a fresh start. Then Peter showed up last week to ask for her forgiveness because he's met someone who made him want to stay sober."

"Oh man, that had to sting."

She nodded. "You're very perceptive."

He took a painful breath and spoke as best he could over the knot in his throat. "The hardest part… is I feel like I've lost my best friend all over again."

Margaret gave him a hug. "Just give her a little time, Jeremy. She'll come around."

CHAPTER 14

Didn't matter how long he walked the beach, the sunset just reminded him more of Cori and their walks along the shore. He missed their camaraderie and closeness. He didn't realize until he didn't have her how much he needed that in his life—a best friend.

With Cori, he felt... encouraged, supported, accompanied. He chuckled at the word but could think of nothing better. Now he felt alone and, well, dull. Nothing seemed very important anymore.

Her mother's words replayed in her head for the umpteenth time. Why had Cori kept the truth from him? But then he remembered how he felt when Sheridan broke things off. He thought he'd done everything he could to make her happy, and yet she wasn't. At all. He'd felt like a complete failure for weeks. And kind of ashamed if he was honest with himself.

Which made him clam up. He didn't even want to talk to Stephen about it. He wished he'd prodded a little more—gotten Cori to open up and share some of the burden she carried. The fear she dealt with didn't scare him. Quite the opposite. He wanted to help her overcome it because he saw the amazing woman she truly was.

So why was he walking on the beach instead of figuring out how to win her back? He needed something big to convince her he had her back. That yes, he loved her, but he also cared about her heart and her future.

He stopped in his tracks. The sound of the waves broke into the noise in his head and clarified the one thought he hadn't really *thought*. He loved Cori?

His chest expanded with the deep breath of sea air as he inhaled. And as he released it, the truth settled deep into his mind and connected to what his heart had been trying to tell him all along.

He loved Cori Carter.

AFTER A TRADITIONAL CHRISTMAS morning at her mother's, Corinne went home, dug out the pfeffernuss cookies she'd stowed in the pantry, and flopped on her couch. She didn't want to see or talk to anyone. Netflix Christmas movies would be her best friend for the rest of the day.

The next morning, she went to her office for a few hours even though everyone had the week off. Why not get a jump on the new year? Made sense to her. After all, moving back home was supposed to be her fresh start and her time to finally focus on her career. Jeremy had turned out to be a distraction. Now she could get back on track.

But she found herself thinking about him all the time. She missed her best friend. She missed his smile. She missed him more than she realized she could miss a person. With Jeremy, she felt seen, understood, protected…and chosen.

She dropped her head in her hands. When had she fallen so hard? Fell in love when she should have been guarding her wounded heart against making another poor decision?

She knew she probably overreacted, but at that moment, the years of pain flooded back when she tasted the alcohol on Jeremy's breath. Too many memories—and pain—lingered. How could she step into a relationship like that? No, Jeremy was better off without her. No one needed to take on baggage like hers.

Her phone dinged. A text from Allison, confirming their lunch date tomorrow. She sent back a thumbs-up as she left her office and headed home. Once back at her condo, she thought about going to the beach and taking a walk, but that just reminded her even more of Jeremy and their time together.

She stood in her living room, staring at nothing and trying to figure out what to do with herself. They'd spent almost every evening together either on a fake date or hanging out at the beach that she'd grown accustomed to his company. She needed a distraction, something to get her mind off those gray-green eyes and slow smile. And the way he held her when they danced, or when he kissed her...

Corinne growled and grabbed the television remote. She still had some Christmas movies saved on Hulu. As she scrolled to her list, her phone buzzed.

Her mother. "Hi, Mom."

"What are you doing?"

"Wow, no hello, just right to the interrogation."

Her mother made a snickering sound. "No, that's not why I'm calling. I just wanted to check on you."

"I'm fine, Mom. In fact, I have big plans this evening with Jack Black, Cameron Diaz, Jude Law, and Kate Winslet." Why hadn't she thought to watch her favorite Christmas movie sooner? She cued up *The Holiday*, ready to lose herself in someone else's drama, even if it wasn't real.

"I haven't a clue which friends those are but be sure to invite them to the New Year's Eve party."

"Um, I'm pretty sure they have plans." She grabbed the bag of pfeffernuss and wolfed down a cookie.

"Sorry to hear that, but I'm glad you're coming."

"I didn't say I was going, so just count me out on that one."

"Sorry, dear, I can't. I've already confirmed with the matchmaker that you'll be there and need a date. See you there."

"Mom!" The line went dead. She tossed her phone onto the couch, hit play, and ate another cookie.

CHAPTER 15

Corinne stepped out of her car and with a frustrated grunt, yanked her dress from the tangle it had become around her legs on the drive over. If she'd just told her mother to cancel the date, she'd be home on her comfy couch watching some New Year's Eve show from the comfort of her own home.

She'd found a decent parking space but still had a bit of a walk to the art gallery where her mother held her party every year to boost the local arts and give good friends—and family this year— close proximity to the Pineapple Drop, an old Sarasota custom that mirrored the ball drop in New York.

That part she looked forward to. She hadn't seen it in years and the event had grown enormously in popularity, as the city had expanded into a buzzing metropolis. Once the pineapple came down, she'd dash back to her car and get back to her list of holiday movies. She still hasn't watched her second favorite, *The Last Holiday*. And she needed a little Queen Latifah in her step these days.

She mingled through the front areas, appreciated the art and gave a smile here and there as she searched for her mother. Her stomach did a slight flutter at the thought of meeting this new date—the matchmaker had delicately let her mother know Samuel was looking for someone with fewer complications. Further confirmation that she really didn't like to offer anyone at the moment, so she'd keep things light with this new candidate. Make it clear she came with baggage.

Maybe that would be her new test filter. She laughed at herself.

"What's so funny?"

She spun around. Had she laughed out loud? "Oh, hey, Allie." She gave her friend a hug. "Nothing really, just laughing at my own thoughts. Have you seen my mother?"

Allie pointed toward the back part of the building. "I think she's in the back getting the caterers clear on when to bring out the champagne." She laughed. "They had a small hiccup earlier with the hors d'oeuvres."

She headed the direction Allie pointed, giving Stephen a quick wave as she walked past him. He waved back before darting in the other direction. She slowed her step a moment—Stephen really was acting strange lately. Allie hadn't brought the topic up again, but maybe she needed to prod her friend again for more details. She'd wound up too engrossed in her own drama that she forgot to check in on her friend.

As she neared the back area, her mother grabbed her wrist and tugged her into a side room. "Finally, you're here. Your date is waiting. I think you'll really like him, Corinne."

"Don't get your hopes up, Mom. Okay? I really want to focus on my career and get my head straight this year."

Her mother stopped and pointed to a chair in the middle of the room. Christmas twinkle lights draped the ceiling and a projector sent delicate snowflakes tumbling down the wall she faced.

What in the world was going on? Did her date want to make a big impression or something? Oh, no, maybe he was a local artist or filmmaker. She'd heard they could be quite quirky. The only clue her mother gave was the mischievous gleam in her eyes that matched her smile.

Music started, soft at first but growing in beat. A man in a black suit shot out from behind a partition, his back to her until he spun around with the dramatic stop of the music.

She gasped. "Jeremy?"

❄

He had her full attention. Now if he could pull off the crazy routine and song he'd thrown together with the help of Stephen. Once Allison found out what he was up to, she'd thrown herself in the ring to help with his wooing shenanigans.

Allison stood to his left, ready to pop the tinsel firecracker when he finished with his rap tune. Stephen waited on his right, playing DJ and ready to activate the rest of the visuals he'd created using a Karaoke machine.

Jeremy gave his friend a nod. The music transitioned into a softer beat.

He did his best to impersonate a serenade. "Cori, when I first saw you in the hallway, I didn't know you'd wind up so far away." He snapped his fingers, and the music shifted into a full rap beat. "But now you're back and I'm no slack. We're meant to be, you and me. So take a stand and take my hand. 'Cus my love is true, and it's all for you."

As the music ended with the last beat, confetti burst between them. Hand out, he moved closer... and waited. She sat there, eyes wide open and her mouth to match. But still had said nothing. His excitement and his heart started a sputtering dive. Had he just made a huge fool of himself for nothing?

Tears welled in her eyes as she accepted his hand and allowed him to pull her up. "You did this for me?"

"Yes, I'd do anything for you. Even a ridiculous rap presentation."

"Just like Mr. Barrett." Her tremulous smile made his heart jump.

Maybe he'd succeeded after all. "Yes. You remembered."

"How could I forget?" She let out a short laugh and sniffed. "Are you sure? I come with baggage."

He looked behind her. "Looks pretty manageable to me. Besides, I may have a little of my own." He glanced at the stage production behind him.

She mimicked his gesture. "I'm pretty sure I can handle it."

He brushed a rogue tear from her cheek. "So do I get a passing grade?"

"More than passing." She went up on tiptoe to kiss him.

Although they had a couple hours until midnight, Jeremy thought for sure fireworks had gone off somewhere early as their lips met. And when she leaned away, he was certain he saw the sparkle of their lights exploding in her eyes.

"I love you too, you know?" She squeezed his hand.

"Are you sure?"

"More than sure."

"Good." He snapped his fingers again, and the music restarted with a melody suited for a slow dance. He twirled her slowly into his arms and pulled her close. "Then let's get this show on the road."

A war came between them. Thirty-eight years later, unexpected events bring them back together at Christmas. Will love spark a second time?

Read A Love Meant to Be and find out just how true love can be!

He's fighting with his past. She's sent to show him a future. Will Lexie succeed in her mission, or will Elliott stay trapped in the torment of his previous life?

Sign up for my newsletter and get a free copy of my novella, The First Encounter.

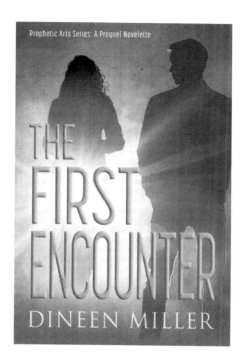

A NOTE FROM DINEEN

Dear friend,

If you enjoyed *The Holiday Arrangement*, please share it with your friends and leave a review on Amazon so other readers can enjoy and enjoy Jeremy and Cori's story too.

Blessings to you!

Dineen

Find me also at DineenMiller.com.

Sign up for my newsletter to get the latest updates on future books, news, and giveaways too!

And please connect with me on these social media platforms:

facebook.com/DineenMiller.AuthorGraphicDesinger

goodreads.com/dineenmiller

twitter.com/dineenmiller

instagram.com/dineenmiller

bookbub.com/authors/dineen-miller

SAMPLE: A LOVE MEANT TO BE

Marcia had dared her, and Gail Gibson never turned down a dare. Her one obvious flaw and probably why her sister had goaded her to check out Mr. Wolfe's apprentice. But the way he returned her gaze gave her mind pause and her heart a jolt. Maybe she was the first redhead he'd ever seen. Or maybe the guy needed to learn it wasn't polite to stare.

Heat rushed to her cheeks, no doubt making her look like a tomato. The bane of her existence. Here she was chastising the poor fellow for staring and she was doing the very same thing. Gail reverted her gaze back to the safety of her sister's ring. "It is gorgeous, Marcia. I hope you told Patrick you love it."

Her sister shrugged. "I told him it was nice."

"Nice? Don't you think he deserves more than that?" Marcia's smile turned into a glare. "He's just trying to appease me because he knows I'm still angry about him signing up for another tour. I'm tired, Gail. I'm tired of raising our kids by myself while the man goes traipsing around jungles and getting drunk with his buddies."

Gail inhaled deeply through her nose. Her sister's moods changed as rapidly as the fashions did these days. She couldn't keep up anymore.

Thankfully she'd be back home after the Christmas break and back to her beloved classes. Books made better companions.

"You should meet him, you know?"

Gail struggled to follow her sister's sudden shift in conversation. "Who?"

Marcia nodded toward the man she'd dared Gail to look at. "Alan James. He's one of Patrick's friends and now a goony for Henry. You two might just hit it off."

"In case you've forgotten, I have a boyfriend."

"Oh yeah, Mr. Wall Street. Better grab him before he finds some cutie ready to play housewife for him."

She glared at her sister. "Troy Pendergast is a good man. He would never do such a thing."

"I bet he doesn't make your heart race like Alan James."

"Marcia, stop it. I will not let you goad me into a fight. I'm very happy with my life, just the way it is."

Marcia stared at her, almost as if she didn't know what to say. But her sister always knew what to say. Just not always the right thing. "A safe boyfriend and stodgy books. Yeah, that sounds downright chipper to me."

Gail thought about Troy. He *was* kind of safe, but she liked that about him. She knew what to expect from him and knew what he expected from her. They were a good fit. She didn't need to be swept off her feet. She smiled. Now was the right time to tell her sister her news. "Troy asked me to marry him before I left."

Marcia grabbed her left hand. "So where's the ring?"

Gail pulled her hand back. Not quite the elation she'd hoped for. "He said he'll have it by the time I get back. That's why he's working for his dad over the holidays."

"Then there's still time."

"Time for what?"

Marcia positioned her body behind Gail's and propelled her forward. "To have one more fling before you settle for Mr. Safe. And Alan James is as good as any fling I've seen lately."

Read A Love Meant to Be and find out just how true love can be!

Printed in Great Britain
by Amazon

76051736R00050